CALGARY PUBLIC LIBRARY
MAR 2016

FRECKLEFACE STRAWBERRY
Loose Tooth!

For kids with loose teeth
—J.M.

 Published in the United States by Doubleday, an imprint of Random House Children's Books, a division of Penguin Random House LLC, New York.

Doubleday and the colophon are registered trademarks of Penguin Random House LLC.

Visit us on the Web! randomhousekids.com

Educators and librarians, for a variety of teaching tools, visit us at RHTeachersLibrarians.com

Library of Congress Cataloging-in-Publication Data
Moore, Julianne.
Freckleface Strawberry : loose tooth! / by Julianne Moore ; illustrated by LeUyen Pham.
pages cm. — (Step into reading. Step 2)
Summary: Freckleface Strawberry wants very much for her first loose tooth to come out while she is at school.
ISBN 978-0-385-39198-6 (hc) — ISBN 978-0-375-97368-0 (glb) — ISBN 978-0-385-39197-9 (pb) — ISBN 978-0-385-39199-3 (ebk)
[1. Teeth—Fiction. 2. Schools—Fiction.] I. Pham, LeUyen, illustrator. II. Title.
III. Title: Loose tooth!.
PZ7.M78635Frn 2016
[E]—dc23
2015001796

MANUFACTURED IN MALAYSIA

10 9 8 7 6 5 4 3 2 1

First Edition

Random House Children's Books supports the First Amendment and celebrates the right to read.

FRECKLEFACE STRAWBERRY
Loose Tooth!

by Julianne Moore
illustrated by LeUyen Pham

Doubleday Books for Young Readers

Chapter 1

Freckleface Strawberry had a loose tooth.

It was her first loose tooth.
It was in the front of
her mouth.

It was very, very loose.
She wanted to lose
the tooth soon.

She did not want to lose it in her room.

She did not want to lose it in the kitchen.

She did not want to lose it on the playground.

She DID want to lose it at school.

Chapter 2

At school,
all the kids would see.
At school,
she could go to the nurse.

At school,
the nurse would give her
a tiny tooth necklace
to wear around her neck.
The necklace was NICE.

Winnie had a necklace.

Windy Pants Patrick
had a necklace.

Noah had a necklace.

Freckleface Strawberry
did not have a necklace.

Chapter 3

Freckleface Strawberry
wiggled her tooth.
She wiggled her tooth
in the classroom.

She wiggled her tooth
in the lunchroom.

She wiggled her tooth
on the jungle gym.

“Freckleface Strawberry,”
said her teacher.
“You are not holding on
with both hands.
Please take your fingers
out of your mouth.”

Windy Pants Patrick said,
"I told you so."

Chapter 4

Freckleface Strawberry
was worried
that she would not get
a tooth necklace.

The day was almost over
and her tooth
had not fallen out.

If she lost her tooth at home,
her mom would not
have a tooth necklace.

Her dad would not
have a tooth necklace.

Her sister had
a tooth necklace,
but she would not
give it to Freckleface.

Freckleface wanted
the necklace.
What could she do?

She was going to have
to do something.
She was going to have
to pull the tooth.
She was going to have
to pull HARD.

“Hey,” said Windy Pants.
“Your tooth just fell out!
You should go to
the nurse.”

And that is how
Freckleface Strawberry
got her tooth necklace.